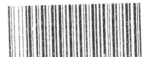

Pooch Parlour

Dog Star

For Holly – KC

For CB and AA, with much appreciation x – JAD

STRIPES PUBLISHING
An imprint of Little Tiger Press
1 The Coda Centre, 189 Munster Road,
London SW6 6AW

This paperback edition first published
in Great Britain in 2014.

ISBN: 978-1-84715-515-3

A CIP catalogue record for this book is available from the British Library.

Printed and bound in the UK.

2 4 6 8 10 9 7 5 3 1

Dog Star

Katy Cannon

Stripes

Chapter One

"Come on, you two." Abi tugged lightly on the leads of the poodles. She was glad that Frosty and Sooty loved Pooch Parlour's Doggy Daycare so much that they didn't want to leave, but it was time for them to go home to their owners!

Beside her, Abi's fluffy little bichon frise, Lulu, gave a small bark. Abi smiled. Lulu knew that once they'd delivered the poodles to Mr and Mrs Harris in reception, she'd get some Barker's Bites as a treat. No wonder she was in a hurry to get them moving.

"See you later, Abi." Rebecca, who ran the Doggy Daycare, waved at them as they left and the door swung shut behind them. Abi liked helping out at the Daycare. There were always lots of interesting new dogs to meet and fun games to play with them. Lulu liked it too – especially if one of the visiting dogs was in a playful mood. The Doggy Daycare had all the best toys – and Abi and Lulu had the whole summer to play with them, while they stayed with Aunt Tiffany.

With the Daycare out of sight, the poodles followed obediently at heel, and Lulu trotted along just behind. As Abi led them down the corridors of her aunt's luxury dog-grooming salon, she passed a few members of Pooch

Parlour staff. They all said hello and most stopped to pat Lulu on the head. Everyone knew how much Lulu liked to be petted.

"Oh, Abi. Great!" Kim bustled down the corridor towards them. "Can you do me a favour, if you're heading to reception? I have to take this message to your aunt, so can you keep an eye on the front desk? I'll be back in two minutes. If anyone comes in, just ask them to take a seat until I get back."

"Of course," Abi said. She pulled the curtain that led into reception to one side and let the dogs go first. Mr and Mrs Harris were already waiting, and Frosty and Sooty barked, rushing forward to greet them.

Abi handed their leads to Mrs Harris with a smile. "They've had a great time," she said.

"Oh, I'm so glad," Mrs Harris said. "I do worry when I have to leave them, but I know they're in good hands here at Pooch Parlour."

Abi waved the Harrises off through the big front window of the salon. As soon as they turned the corner, Lulu placed her paws on Abi's leg, almost standing up, and Abi laughed. "Don't worry, Lulu, I haven't forgotten about your Barker's Bites! When Kim gets back, we'll go and find some."

Just then, the front door opened. Abi and Lulu headed to the reception desk and smiled at the newcomers – a tall man in jeans and a T-shirt, and a girl around Abi's age carrying a tiny Yorkshire terrier puppy.

"Welcome to Pooch Parlour," Abi said politely.

The man raised his eyebrows. "Aren't you a little young to be working here?" he asked with a grin.

"I'm just helping out for the summer," Abi explained. "Kim – that's the receptionist – will be back any second." What else had Kim told her to say? Abi glanced round the room and spotted the long, velvet sofa beside the desk. That was it! "Would you like to take a seat until she gets back?"

"Actually, I have an appointment with Tiffany," the man said, not sitting down. Instead, he started pacing round the reception area, picking up catalogues and leaflets, flicking through them quickly then putting them back down again. "My name is Don Francis. I'm a film director."

Abi's eyes widened. She knew that name! Don Francis was the director of the *Barking Mad* movies, starring Pooch Parlour's most famous client, Daisy Lane. She wondered if Daisy had recommended them.

"And I'm Polly," the girl said, settling on to the sofa. "His daughter. And this is Pickle," she added, pointing at the Yorkie.

"I'm Abi and this is Lulu."

Lulu barked at her name and padded over to Pickle. The two little dogs sniffed round each other, darting back and forth, neither quite sure what to make of the other. Lulu had grown used to being round a lot of new dogs since they'd arrived at Pooch Parlour, but Abi didn't know how well Pickle played with strangers.

She waited, a little nervously, until Lulu's tail began to wag, the whole back half of her body wiggling with excitement. Pickle's tail started to move too, and the tiny Yorkie yapped and nuzzled Lulu's side.

Abi smiled at Polly. "I'll just go and fetch Aunt Tiffany," she said, happy to leave Lulu with her new friend.

She rushed towards the curtain that led to the Pooch Parlour offices, but paused before she went through. Turning round, she saw Mr Francis inspecting a display of dog brushes by the counter.

"Um, Mr Francis..." He looked up, and Abi took a breath. "I just wanted to say ... I really love your films!"

The words came out in a rush, and Abi bit her lip as soon as she'd blurted them out. She shouldn't be bothering a famous film director!

But Mr Francis grinned at her. "Well, that's good news," he said, "because I'm making one just round the corner from here."

Abi gasped. "*Really?*" It was too exciting for words!

"Really," Mr Francis said with a nod. "It's called *Sally White and the Seven Dogs.* And what's more, I'm here today to see if we can use Pooch Parlour for the dogs' grooming before we start filming!"

Chapter Two

Abi skipped through the corridors towards Aunt Tiffany's office. She was so excited about telling her aunt that Mr Francis had arrived that she almost didn't see Kim coming the other way.

"Abi, what's happened? Did someone come in?" Kim asked.

Abi nodded. "Don Francis, the director! He says he has an appointment with Aunt Tiffany."

Kim's eyes widened. "Oh wow! He's early!

I'd better go and welcome him. Can you fetch your aunt?"

Abi nodded, and Kim hurried off.

Aunt Tiffany's office was at the back of the building, next to the training room and the party room. Abi knocked on the door and, when her aunt called out, she stuck her head into the room. "Aunt Tiffany! Don Francis is here! He says he has a meeting with you."

The slight lifting of Aunt Tiffany's eyebrows was the only sign that she was surprised. Sliding back her chair, she picked up the neatly organized file from the desk. "Already? Gosh, he's early. Most film types I've dealt with tend to keep you waiting."

Abi thought about the director, fiddling with everything on display in reception. "I think he gets bored easily," she said. "Maybe *he* got bored of waiting."

"Probably." Aunt Tiffany ran a hand over her blonde hair. "How do I look?"

"Perfect," Abi said with a smile. Aunt Tiffany always looked fabulous, even when they were in their pyjamas drinking hot chocolate and watching TV on a Saturday night. It was funny to think that even Aunt Tiffany might be just a little bit nervous about meeting Don Francis.

"He's brought his daughter, Polly, with him," Abi told her, as they hurried towards reception. Aunt Tiffany's miniature dachshund, Hugo, scampered to keep up with them, his soft ears flapping. "And Polly's brought her dog."

"That's nice. Maybe you and Lulu can help keep Polly entertained while Mr Francis and I talk about what he needs from Pooch Parlour."

"Yes! I can do that!" Abi said. Polly seemed nice, she thought, and Pickle and Lulu were already getting along.

"Mr Francis," Aunt Tiffany said, beaming, as they walked into reception. "Sorry to keep you waiting."

The director had found a display cabinet of glittery dog collars to peer at, while Polly was reading one of the magazines that Kim left out for visitors.

"You must be Tiffany," he said, turning away from the display. "And don't worry. Your lovely receptionist brought me a coffee."

Behind the reception desk, Kim looked at the floor and grinned shyly.

Mr Francis lifted his cup to his lips and drank the rest of his coffee, before placing the empty cup back on the tray in front of Kim. Polly did the same with her glass of squash.

"And now, I'm ready for the grand tour," Mr Francis said.

"Then let's get to it." Aunt Tiffany opened the door that led to the rest of Pooch Parlour and held it for him to walk through.

Abi and Lulu waited for Polly and Pickle before following the two adults. "You're with me," Abi said with a smile.

"Oh good!" Polly replied. "I wanted to ask you about your gorgeous dog."

"And I wanted to ask you about your dad's film!"

"Oh, don't worry," Polly said, as they headed through the door. "You'll hear all about that. He hasn't talked about anything else for *months*."

"The film is called *Sally White and the Seven Dogs*," Mr Francis told Aunt Tiffany. "It's a retelling of the Snow White story, but with dogs."

"What breeds of dogs do you have in it?" Abi asked, as they reached the Doggy Spa. Mr Francis seemed to like answering questions about his film, which made her less nervous about asking them. "And where do you find them?"

"They're highly trained, professional dog actors, provided by my canine casting agency." For some reason, Mr Francis looked at Polly as he said this, and she pulled a face. "For this film, we have a Labrador, a Great Dane, a bulldog, a malamute, a spaniel, a Border collie and a Yorkshire terrier."

"Pickle?" Abi guessed.

"No," Mr Francis said. "Not Pickle." He turned to Aunt Tiffany. "So, this is the grooming parlour?"

"Yes, this is the Doggy Spa. Let me show you…"

As Aunt Tiffany gave Mr Francis the tour, Abi turned to Polly. "It's a shame Pickle's not in the film," Abi said. She knelt down to pet the tiny Yorkie. "She's so cute!"

Lulu butted up against her hand too, not wanting to be left out.

"I know." Polly sighed. "Dad's given me a really small part in the film, right at the beginning. I wanted Pickle to be in it with me, but Dad said no."

"Why?" Abi asked. At the same time she was thinking how amazing it was that Polly got to be in the film. She was so lucky to have a famous dad! Abi wasn't jealous, though. She'd rather be behind the scenes, training the dogs, than starring on the big screen.

"He says that Pickle's not professionally trained," Polly explained. "But she's been practising with the agency dogs and she's really good!"

"Come on, girls," Aunt Tiffany called. "We're off to see the Doggy Daycare next."

"Pickle will like this room," Abi told Polly. "It's where all the best toys are!" Pickle woofed her approval at the word "toys".

By the time they'd seen the Doggy Daycare, the Doggy Den, where the dogs went for a snooze when they were tired of playing, the wardrobe room, the party room, the training room, where Aunt Tiffany gave obedience classes every Saturday morning, and the studio, where Jason, the Pooch Parlour photographer, took photos for dog portraits, Mr Francis had a broad grin on his face.

"I think your dad likes it here," Abi whispered to Polly, as Mr Francis helped himself to the fresh coffee Kim brought in the moment they returned to reception.

"So does Pickle," Polly said, pointing to where Pickle and Lulu were playing together with a squeaky bone toy they'd picked up. "And so do I."

Abi smiled. It was nice to have someone her own age at Pooch Parlour. If Mr Francis chose Pooch Parlour as the grooming parlour for his film, maybe Polly would get to visit during filming too.

"Well, I think I've seen all I need to see," Mr Francis said, flicking through the Pooch Parlour brochure Aunt Tiffany had given him and stirring his coffee with his other hand.

"I hope you've seen that the Pooch Parlour team would take excellent care of your dog stars," Aunt Tiffany replied.

"I certainly have." Mr Francis dropped the brochure on to the counter. "And I think Pooch Parlour will be the perfect Official Grooming Parlour for *Sally White and the Seven Dogs.*"

Abi and Polly cheered, while Lulu and Pickle both looked up and barked.

But then Mr Francis's mobile phone rang.

"Hello?" he said, answering it. "Wait. What? What do you mean it's *cancelled*?"

Chapter Three

"That doesn't sound good," Polly whispered to Abi. "People don't usually cancel on Dad."

Abi nodded, watching Mr Francis pace across the reception area, his phone pressed to his ear. Every now and then he'd nod, or say "But—" in a sharp voice. It was hard to imagine anyone telling a famous director "No", but apparently it had happened.

Lulu, Hugo and Pickle sat in the middle of the floor, their heads turning as they watched Mr Francis walk up and down. Aunt Tiffany frowned, and Abi bit her lip as they all waited for Mr Francis to finish his call and tell them what was happening. The tension made it feel like the whole room was being pulled tighter and tighter, until it might snap in two!

"Well then, I will just have to fix it, won't I?" Mr Francis stabbed the "end call" button on his phone and turned to face them. "It seems that *Woof!* magazine have a problem with the venue for tomorrow's photo shoot."

Polly gasped. "Oh no!"

"Is this a promotion for the film?" Aunt Tiffany asked.

"It was *the* promotion," Mr Francis said, turning his phone over and over in his hands. "This photo shoot was supposed to introduce the dog stars to the public, and I was going to give an interview about the film. We had the most incredible place lined up – a stately home with a huge glass conservatory full of trees and plants. But apparently there was a storm last night and some of the panes of glass were broken, so it's not safe for us to use. They want to postpone until it's fixed, or until they can find another venue, but by then we'll have started filming properly and there won't be time..."

What a disaster! Abi looked over at her new friend. Polly looked so upset, and even Pickle had put her head down on her paws.

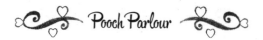

"What are you going to do?" Abi asked.

"What am I going to do," Mr Francis repeated. "What *am* I going to do? What am I going to *do*?"

He sounded like he was thinking about it very hard. Then, all of a sudden, he dropped his phone into his pocket. "I'll tell you what I'm going to do. No, what *we're* going to do. We're going to have the photo shoot right here!"

"Yes!" Polly said, grabbing Abi's hands. "It'll be perfect!"

But Aunt Tiffany didn't seem so sure. "Here? But—"

"Where else?" Mr Francis gave her a wide grin. "You have the party room – that will give us the space, and my guys can make it look every bit as fabulous as some conservatory. And we can have all the dogs groomed and primped here beforehand. It's ideal!"

"But … tomorrow?" Aunt Tiffany said. "We have other clients booked in…"

Abi slipped behind the reception desk and pulled out the appointment book. "Aunt Tiffany's right. We're fully booked. They're all regulars too." It was funny how fast she'd come to recognize the names of their most regular clients – owners and dogs.

"Reschedule them!" Mr Francis peered over Abi's shoulder at the book, pointing at the appointments they had scheduled for the next day. "I bet if you offer them tickets to the premiere of *Sally White and the Seven Dogs* they won't mind one bit."

Abi's eyes widened. A film premiere! With the red carpet and the fancy dresses and the stars and the cameras… Wow! She wondered if she and Aunt Tiffany might get to go too. Maybe even Lulu! She could have a special outfit…

But Aunt Tiffany still didn't seem sure. "I'll need to call everyone first."

"Great! Then that's settled." Mr Francis drained his cup of coffee. "I'll contact my PR person, and get them to come over here for a meeting. Meanwhile, Polly and I had better get back to the film set, and see how the dogs settling in."

Abi sighed. She wished *she* could go and see the professional dogs and their trainers.

But then, as if her silent wish had been heard, Polly said, "Dad? Can Abi and Lulu come with us for a visit?"

Abi held her breath as they waited for an answer...

Chapter Four

Mr Francis looked at Abi, then at Lulu. "I don't see why not. As long as Tiffany doesn't mind."

"Great!" Polly said, clapping her hands together gleefully.

"Please, Aunt Tiffany?" Abi bounced on her toes. "Can I go?"

Aunt Tiffany laughed. "Yes, go on then. It looks like I'm going to be pretty tied up here, anyway! I'll come and collect you when we close for the day, if that's OK with Mr Francis?"

She glanced over at Polly's dad, who nodded. "And I'll need you back here tomorrow to help get everything set up," she added.

"Of course!" Abi grinned. She didn't want to miss out on helping get Pooch Parlour ready for the photo shoot. And if she got to know the dogs that afternoon, she'd be even more useful tomorrow when they all needed grooming and looking after.

But right now she was going to see a real, proper film set – with professional dog actors and trainers. This was a chance to see her dream career in action!

Mr Francis drove them to the park where they were setting up for filming, then left the girls and their dogs with his assistant, Greta, for a tour. But just moments after he left,

Greta got a phone call.

"Will you girls be OK for a few minutes while I take this?" Greta asked, and Polly and Abi nodded.

"Don't worry," Polly said. "Pickle and I already know our way around – we can give Abi the tour!"

Abi couldn't help but stare as Polly showed her the film set. They were still setting up, but already there seemed to be people everywhere, all rushing from one place to another and calling out to each other. Abi could only imagine how much busier it would be when they started filming in a couple of days.

Lulu stuck close to Abi's side, but Abi kept a tight grip on her lead, just in case. Lulu was very well behaved, usually, but if something separated them, it could take forever to find the little dog again amongst all this activity.

"There's the catering van, that's the trailer for the actress playing Sally White..."

Polly waved her arms around, pointing out everything so quickly that Abi could barely keep up. She supposed that for Polly, being on a film set was perfectly ordinary. For Abi and Lulu, it was all a bit overwhelming!

"And this is what you really want to see!" Polly stopped and grinned at Abi. There, in front of them, were seven dogs, each being led around a short obstacle course by their handlers. They weaved between posts, crawled through tunnels and jumped over low bars, all perfectly in time. It was incredible!

As they watched, the seven dogs lined up at the end of the course and were rewarded by their handlers with biscuits and lots of praise and petting. They all looked very pleased with themselves.

The head trainer announced a break and one of the handlers, a young woman, headed towards where Abi and Polly were standing. She had two of the dogs with her – a Great Dane and a bulldog – and they both followed at her heels on their leads.

"Hi, Polly," she said, smiling at them both. "I see you've made some new friends." She gave Pickle a quick pat, then turned her attention to Lulu, who rolled on her back to have her tummy stroked. "Aren't you a beauty?" She looked up at Abi. "I love the way bichon frise coats spring under your fingers. What's her name?"

"Lulu," Abi said. "And I'm Abi."

"Abi's aunt runs the grooming parlour that Dad's using for the film," Polly explained. "And for the photo shoot tomorrow, apparently!"

"Pooch Parlour, right? Great. Then we'll be seeing a lot more of you." She held out a hand. "I'm Fran. And these boys are Duke and Frank." She nodded at the Great Dane and the bulldog in turn. "I'm in charge of Duke, and Kirsty, the woman talking to the AD over there," – she pointed over at where a woman was talking to a man with a clipboard – "she's in charge of Frank."

"AD?" Abi whispered to Polly.

"Assistant Director," Polly replied.

"The AD is in charge of us handlers – and the dog stars, of course," Fran said. "We're all from the same agency on this film, which makes things easier. Each dog has a handler. Sometimes it's the dog's actual owner, but most of us are hired by the agency." She ran a hand over Duke's head. "Luckily for us, they're all very well trained."

"They looked great out there," Abi said, a little shyly.

"They've been working very hard, getting ready for this film," Fran said.

Polly let out Pickle's lead a little so the tiny Yorkie could get closer to the big dogs. "Pickle's been training with them too."

"And she's coming along nicely. You should get her registered with the agency, Polly.

Soon she could be starring in her own films!"

Fran looked down at Lulu, who stuck close to Pickle as they sniffed around Duke and Frank. "What about this little lady? Has she had any training?"

Abi nodded. "I've been training her myself. And she takes part in the obedience classes at Pooch Parlour on a Saturday."

Lulu was getting very good at knowing what Abi wanted her to do. But she had a long way to go to reach the same standard as the dog actors.

"Well, why don't we see what these two can do then?" Fran said, as the head trainer called everyone back. "Looks like we're starting again. We're only running a basic course right now – I bet no one would mind if Pickle and Lulu joined in. One of the reasons we're here today is so the dogs can get used to the location and all the activity. What do you think?"

Abi looked over at Polly, who was practically jumping about with excitement. It looked like they were all about to find out just how good Lulu's training was…

"OK then," Abi said. "Let's go!"

Chapter Five

Fran went to talk to the head trainer, who nodded as she spoke. Turning, Fran gave the girls a thumbs up, so Abi and Polly led Lulu and Pickle out to where the other dogs were lining up with their handlers.

"Are you sure about this?" Abi whispered to Polly.

"It'll be fine!" Polly grinned at her. "Besides, don't you want to prove that our dogs are every bit as good as the professionals?"

"Yeah, I guess so!" Abi smiled at Polly's confidence. The girls ordered their dogs to stand and wait for the commands to start.

Abi and Lulu were at the back of the line, just behind Polly and Pickle, so even if they didn't get it right, they wouldn't be holding anyone up.

Fran went first, leading Duke through the poles. Abi was amazed that such a big dog could weave so elegantly. She hoped Lulu could do it as well!

After Duke went Frank with Kirsty, then a Labrador, a wolf-like malamute, a cute spaniel and a shaggy Border collie. When the seventh dog ran forward, Abi blinked and checked that Polly was still next to her – the seventh dog looked exactly like Pickle!

There was no time to whisper this to Polly, though, as it was the real Pickle's turn next. Abi waited until Pickle had made it through all the poles without stopping, and moved on to the tunnel, before leading Lulu forward.

Off her lead, Abi had to trust Lulu to stay close and do as she asked her. Fortunately, Lulu was used to doing the pole exercise at the Pooch Parlour classes and managed to weave her way through with no problems. She hesitated in front of the tunnel, but a few encouraging words from Abi got her to go in, tail wagging behind her as she padded along. Then came the bars, which were tiny hurdles for dogs. The larger dogs had tackled higher ones, but Pickle and the other Yorkshire terrier had jumped lower ones, which is where Abi led Lulu.

"Up, Lulu," Abi said, raising her hand to show Lulu the sign for "jump". But Lulu carried on and ran around the first barrier. Abi felt disappointed, but there were still two more hurdles to go – she wouldn't give up yet!

"Come on, Lulu! Up!" Abi put as much enthusiasm and excitement into her voice as she could, and this time Lulu jumped the hurdle! "Good girl!" Running alongside her, Abi led Lulu to the next hurdle and called for her to jump again – and she did!

"Well done, Lulu!" Abi knelt down beside the fluffy white dog and wrapped her arms around her. She was so proud of her. Lulu was every bit as much of a star as the professionals. Maybe one day, they'd both get to work on films together!

"Did you see Pickle?" Polly asked, dashing over, with her tiny Yorkie following at her heels.

"She had a perfect run – first time ever!"

"That's fantastic," Abi said. "And Lulu did really well for her first time on a new course."

Fran came over and handed Abi a small bag of dog treats. "They were both great. You'd better reward them, so they know what a good job they did. Rewards are the most important part of dog training."

"Oh, I know," Abi replied. Lulu barked her excitement as Abi offered her a treat. "And she deserves every one. She's a star!"

Once Pickle and Lulu had eaten their treats, Polly and Abi clipped them back on to their leads and took them across the park, a little bit away from the hustle and bustle of the set.

"So, what's your part in the film, then?" Abi asked as they walked.

"Oh, I've only got a couple of lines," Polly said. "I'm the little girl that Sally White meets in the park, right at the beginning of the film. We talk for a minute, and I warn her that there are all sorts of creepy stories about the woods. She says she has to go into them anyway because her dog has run away. Then I wave her goodbye as she walks into the trees." Polly shrugged. "That's it."

Polly made it sound like nothing, but Abi thought it sounded exciting! "You get to be in a real film! That's so amazing."

"Yes, it is." Polly smiled. "But I wish Pickle could be in it too. I thought it would be great if I was walking Pickle in the park when I met Sally White."

"That makes sense," Abi said. "So what's the problem?"

"Dad says Pickle's not a properly trained dog actor, so we can't risk using her." Polly kicked at a stone on the path. "But you saw her! She can do everything the dog stars can do. She'd be great in the film."

An idea started to form in Abi's head. This could be a brilliant chance for her to test her training skills… "Well, in that case, we'll just have to prove to your dad that Pickle is every bit as good as those other dogs!"

Chapter Six

By the time Aunt Tiffany came to collect Abi from the set that evening, the girls had worked out a plan. Polly giggled as they said goodbye, and Abi reminded her that they were meeting at Pooch Parlour at eight the next morning.

"Sounds good to me," Aunt Tiffany said. "We'll need all hands on deck to get things ready for the photo shoot. Polly, you can help Abi, if you like."

Polly nodded. "I will!" Then she leaned closer to Abi and whispered, "Don't forget your research project for tonight."

"Oh, I won't," Abi promised. This was her big chance. She wasn't going to think about anything else until Pickle had a part in Mr Francis's film!

Back at Aunt Tiffany's flat that evening, Abi and Lulu curled up on the bed in Abi's candy-striped room and started researching.

Flicking through the book she'd brought from home – *Doggy Details: How to Care for Your Dog* – Abi found the section on training and started to read. Lulu poked her head over the top of the pages and woofed.

"Do you want to learn this stuff too, Lulu?" Abi asked, shifting to make room for the little dog beside her.

Lulu wriggled into the space, her fluffy body warm against Abi's side.

Abi skipped through the pages covering things she'd seen Pickle do on the film set that day. She already knew how to obey basic commands like "jump", and Polly said she knew "sit" and "stay", as well as "fetch". But they needed something a bit more unusual to impress Mr Francis.

So when she came to the page titled "Great Tricks to Teach Your Dog", Abi started reading much more carefully.

Dogs respond well to rewards, the book said. *If you want to teach your dog some simple tricks, the first thing to do is stock up on doggy treats!*

Not a problem at Pooch Parlour, Abi thought. They had plenty of snacks and treats there.

When you're ready to start—

"Abi?" Aunt Tiffany called from the other room. "Dinner's ready."

Abi closed the book. She'd read the rest after dinner. And then she'd be ready to share everything she'd learned with Polly and Pickle tomorrow.

The next morning Aunt Tiffany and Abi arrived at Pooch Parlour earlier than ever before, but the whole place was already buzzing with activity.

"How are you getting on with rescheduling the appointments, Kim? Did you manage to get hold of everyone we couldn't talk to yesterday?" Aunt Tiffany stowed her handbag behind the reception desk and hung up her jacket.

Abi unclipped Lulu and Hugo from their leads and Hugo padded off towards the shimmering curtain that led to the offices – and to his dog bed in Aunt Tiffany's office. Hugo didn't like a lot of fuss and bother, and there was likely to be plenty of both at Pooch Parlour that day.

Kim looked up from the appointments book with a tired smile. "Getting there! Just two more to go."

"Is everybody OK with having their appointments rearranged?" Aunt Tiffany asked.

"I think so. Most of them were thrilled to hear they'd get to go to a Don Francis movie premiere! Apparently they're not easy to get into – even for some of our more famous clients."

Just then, the front door opened again, and Mr Francis and Polly walked in, with Pickle scampering along behind.

Aunt Tiffany's eyes widened. "Mr Francis! We weren't expecting you until later."

Polly's dad grinned. "Don't worry. The dogs

won't be here for a while – except Pickle," he added, and the little Yorkie barked at the sound of her name. "I just wanted to run through some of the details with you before you get too busy prepping the dogs."

"Of course," Aunt Tiffany said. "Why don't we go through to my office. Abi, I'm sure you and Polly can entertain yourselves. Is that OK?"

Abi nodded. "We'll find something to do, Aunt Tiffany," she said, keeping her face serious, even though she wanted to jump with excitement. This was the perfect opportunity for them to train Pickle!

Polly giggled then slapped a hand over her mouth to stop herself.

Kim gave them a funny look, but luckily Aunt Tiffany and Mr Francis had already disappeared through the curtain.

"What are you two up to?" Kim asked,

raising an eyebrow. "You're both looking far too mischievous for my liking."

"Don't worry, Kim," Abi said. "We're not doing anything we shouldn't be. We're just going to go and get Pickle and Lulu ready for this afternoon."

Kim didn't look convinced. "Well just make sure that whatever you're doing, you tidy up after yourselves."

"We will," Abi and Polly said at the same time. Then they laughed as they set off towards the training room, with Pickle and Lulu close behind.

This was going to be the best surprise Mr Francis had ever had!

Chapter Seven

The training room was empty, just as Abi had known it would be. Everyone was far too busy getting ready for the photo shoot, and there were no other dogs at the parlour today except for Hugo. Not until the dog stars arrived, anyway.

"So, what do we do?" Polly asked, sitting cross-legged on the floor. "I've only ever done training in classes, or with the handlers on film sets."

"It's pretty much the same thing," Abi said as she pulled her book out of her rucksack and set it on the floor between them. "Except we're the teachers. My mum gave me this book when I got Lulu. There are some really good tricks in it. I think we should start by getting Pickle and Lulu to shake hands with us, then maybe we can work up to a high five. Or even train them to wave on command!"

The girls leaned over the book, reading the instructions, while Lulu and Pickle nosed their way in, snuffling at the pages.

"So, first we need treats?" Polly asked, when she'd finished reading.

Abi nodded. "And luckily, I know just where Aunt Tiffany keeps them!"

"Won't she mind?" Polly looked a little nervous, but Abi quickly reassured her.

"Not at all. She told me that I could use this

room – and the rewards – whenever I wanted to practise with Lulu."

Polly's face brightened. "Oh good. My dad would never let Pickle be in the film if we got in trouble with your aunt!"

Abi crossed the room and opened the special cupboard where Aunt Tiffany kept all the doggy treats. She picked up the biggest bag she could find. She'd watched some training videos on Aunt Tiffany's laptop after dinner last night, and the trainers all used an awful lot of biscuits!

"OK," Abi said, setting down the bag of treats on a table that was just high enough that the dogs couldn't reach it. "Here's the plan. I'll do the movement with Lulu first, then you can follow and do the same with Pickle."

Polly nodded enthusiastically. "Let's get started!"

"First we hold out a treat for them to smell."

Abi put a biscuit in the palm of her hand, covered it with her thumb, and held it out to Lulu. The treats Aunt Tiffany used for training were small but chewy – she said that was so the dogs didn't eat too many, or eat them too quickly.

Lulu nuzzled against her hand, trying to get at the treat, but Abi held it just out of reach.

"This is how we taught Pickle other commands," Polly said, holding a treat out to Pickle. "Like 'sit', and 'stay'."

The next step was for the dogs to reach up with their paws to touch the hand holding the treat. As soon as Lulu's paw came up to Abi's hand she made a big fuss of the fluffy dog.

"That's it, Lulu! Shake hands! Good girl!" Then Abi gave her a treat from the bag using her other hand. "The book says it's important to give the treat with your other hand," Abi said, as Pickle started to paw at Polly's hand. "I guess that's because they need to learn to do it without us holding the treat at all."

Polly nodded and reached out for a treat with her other hand too, and rewarded Pickle.

"So, what's next?" Polly asked.

"Now we do this over and over again until they can do it without the treats."

Polly pulled a face. "Teaching dogs tricks takes a long time, doesn't it?"

"Yep." Abi smiled to herself. It was a slow process and it could be hard work, but she enjoyed it. "Won't it be worth it when Pickle gets to be in the film?"

"I guess so!" Polly grinned. "Let's get to work."

It took the girls a while, but eventually Pickle and Lulu could both shake hands on command, and although Abi and Polly still made a fuss over them when they got it right, they didn't need a treat every time.

They'd just moved on to getting the dogs to wave – which was just like shaking hands, really, except the dogs pawed at the air instead of the girls' hands – when they heard voices outside.

"The other dogs must be here!" Abi jumped to her feet. "Come on, we'd better go and help Aunt Tiffany."

Polly's mouth drooped with disappointment. "But Pickle still hasn't managed to wave properly," she said. "She keeps pawing my hand instead."

"We'll practise some more later," Abi promised. "Besides, we can still show your dad that Pickle can shake hands."

"I suppose," Polly said, unconvinced.

The girls raced towards reception, past delivery men bringing in all sorts of boxes and equipment to the party room. Abi couldn't wait to find out what was in them all. Or to show Mr Francis Pickle's new trick.

But then they reached reception.

Fran and Kirsty were there, along with a few of the other handlers from the set, and Mr Francis, Aunt Tiffany and the whole Pooch Parlour staff. With the seven dog stars, plus Pickle, Lulu and Hugo, the room was very crowded!

The adults were all strangely silent, and even the dogs were quiet. Abi was about to ask what was going on, when she realized what everyone was staring at.

There, in the centre of the room, stood the smallest of the dog stars – the little Yorkshire terrier that looked just like Pickle.

And he'd had a haircut.

Chapter Eight

"What happened to him?" Polly whispered, as they all stared at the tiny Yorkie.

The tiny Yorkie with bald patches.

"Apparently his owner's kids decided that Fidget needed a haircut before his big photo shoot." Mr Francis spat the words out. He was sitting in the corner of the room with his head in his hands as he stared at the smallest dog star. Hugo lay at his feet, velvety ears flopped down, looking almost as depressed as the director.

Abi had never seen Mr Francis so still before. She definitely didn't think now was the right time to show him Pickle's new trick.

"Can you fix it?" Abi asked Aunt Tiffany, moving to her aunt's side.

Aunt Tiffany winced, but crouched down next to Fidget and ran a hand over his coat.

"How about putting him in a really cute outfit?" Mel, the wardrobe mistress suggested, but Mr Francis just kept glaring at Fidget.

Aunt Tiffany stood up again. "The best I can do is even out the cut so the bald spots aren't as noticeable."

"But they'll still show up in the photos, right?" Mr Francis said.

"Probably," Aunt Tiffany admitted. "I'm sorry, I don't know what else to suggest."

Everyone stood around looking glum, while in the centre of the room Fidget played with his little bone-shaped chew toy. Pickle and Lulu approached, wanting to play, too. Abi stared at them. Pickle and Fidget really did look very alike – except for the haircut…

Suddenly, Mr Francis jumped to his feet. "Right! Greta, call the animal casting agency. See if we can get our second Yorkie choice for the first few days of filming. In the meantime" – he turned to Polly and Abi – "you two help get all the dogs ready for their photos – including Pickle."

"Really?" Polly gasped. She threw her arms around her dad and gave him a big hug. "Thank you, thank you, thank you!"

"It's just for the photo shoot," Mr Francis warned and Polly nodded, still beaming. "She can be Fidget's stand-in, just for today."

"For now, anyway," Abi whispered to Polly as the girls led Lulu and Pickle towards the Doggy Spa. After all, Mr Francis hadn't seen Pickle's new trick yet.

The Doggy Spa was packed with people – and dogs! Every Pooch Parlour groomer had been called in to get the dog stars ready. First, the dogs would be combed and brushed to remove loose hairs. Then their coats would be trimmed, before the groomers handed them over to be bathed.

"Abi, can you show Polly how to help the dogs choose their bubbles?" Mel asked. "Then we need you over here to help with the shampooing."

"OK!" Abi took Polly over to the shelves of bottles at the far side of the room. "Right, here's what you do. Every dog gets to choose their own bubble bath."

"Really?" Polly looked at the shelves and shelves of bottles. "There are hundreds of them! How do they pick?"

"We choose three and let the dogs sniff them," Abi explained. "It's usually pretty obvious which one they like best. Think you can manage it?"

Polly nodded, even though she didn't look completely certain. But Abi was sure she'd be fine once she got started.

Polly seemed to manage well and each dog arrived at the bath with their handler holding a bottle of bubble bath. Abi drained the bone-shaped tub each time, and poured the bubbles into the fresh water. It was a good job they only used shallow baths for the dogs, or it would have taken forever!

Abi thought it was exciting to wash and clean so many different dogs. They were mostly very well behaved – she supposed they must be used to strangers grooming them. Still, it was funny to go from washing Pickle, a tiny Yorkie, to shampooing Duke, the enormous Great Dane who took up the whole tub! Lulu sat at her side the whole time, looking like she wished it was her turn for a bath.

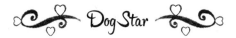

"Tomorrow, Lulu, I'll give you a lovely long bath, with lots of your favourite bubbles," Abi promised.

Abi took her time with each dog. Aunt Tiffany liked her customers to feel pampered, and Abi knew it was important that they all look sparkling clean and perfect for the photo shoot. With the dogs that enjoyed the bath it was easy – she told them how good they were, and they were happy to let her rub the shampoo through their fur then rinse it off with the handheld shower attached to the bath.

But Charlie, the spaniel, didn't like baths. Not one bit.

"Come on, boy, it's just a bit of water." Abi said soothingly as she held him. But Charlie kept wriggling and slipping through her hands as she tried to rinse him off. Eventually, Abi turned off the shower and Charlie stopped moving, just for a moment.

"Is it the shower that you don't like?" Abi asked. "How about this then?" She picked up a flannel from the side of the bath, dunked it in the water and squeezed it out. Then, very gently, she wiped Charlie's face clean, taking care not to get water in his big dark eyes or floppy ears. "That's better, isn't it?"

"Abi?" Aunt Tiffany called from across the room. "Is Charlie ready yet?"

"Just finished," Abi called back. Time for the next customer!

Eventually, all seven dogs had been washed, shampooed and rinsed, then handed back over to the groomers to be dried, first using fluffy towels, then under the special Doggy Dryers. After that, they had their nails clipped, ears and eyes cleaned, and final tidy-ups.

Abi dried her hands on a towel then looked for Polly. Her new friend was watching Pickle have her nails clipped. But before Abi could go over, Aunt Tiffany appeared in the doorway.

"Abi? Polly? If you're finished here, I've got another special job for you…"

Chapter Nine

"Mr Francis wants each of the dogs to have a matching red collar," Aunt Tiffany said as Pickle jumped down from the grooming table. "He's had these tags made with each of their character names on. Do you think you girls can find seven collars in the wardrobe room to fit the dogs?"

"Of course," Abi said.

The wardrobe room was packed full of outfits, collars, bows and costumes. Seven red collars should be no problem at all.

Aunt Tiffany handed over a small bag, the tags jingling inside, and a piece of paper with all the dogs' neck measurements on. "Thanks, girls. Meet us in the party room when you're ready. It's almost time for the photo shoot to start!"

Polly had seen the wardrobe room on their tour of Pooch Parlour earlier that week, but she still stared round the room with wide eyes when they walked in. "There are so many outfits in here!" she gasped. "How are we ever going to find anything?"

Abi smiled. She'd felt the same the first time she'd had to put together an outfit in the wardrobe room. But now she knew she could find anything she needed.

Lulu was perfectly at home too. She padded straight off to look at some of the fancy-dress outfits Mel had on display, Pickle following behind.

"It's easy," Abi told Polly, trying to sound reassuring. "Well, as long as you know how Mel organizes all the clothes, which I do. Come on – collars are this way."

Mel kept the collars next to the fitting rooms. There were a few on display, but most were in colour-coded drawers. "All we have to do is pull out the red drawer!"

Abi opened the drawer. Together, the girls sorted through the collars to find seven that looked the same, ranging in size from a tiny one for Pickle to one large enough to fit Wolf, the malamute with the bushy fur. Hooking each tag on to a collar, they were soon ready to head over to the photo shoot.

"I wish we had more time to look at the clothes," Polly said, as they were leaving. "I bet there are some perfect Pickle outfits in there." She pointed over to where Lulu was pawing at a bee costume on a rail of doggy fancy-dress outfits.

Pickle, meanwhile, had found a basket full of ribbons and tipped them on to the floor.

"Maybe your dad will let you come and choose one another day?" Abi suggested, as she tidied up the ribbons. "Pickle and Lulu could give us a fashion show!"

Polly grinned. "Definitely!"

Abi picked a bright red bow to match the collar and swapped it with the green one in Pickle's topknot. "There," she said. "*Now* we're ready for the photo shoot!"

The party room was right next to the training room they'd used that morning. Usually it looked pretty plain, unless it was decked out with streamers and flags for a doggy birthday party. Today, it barely looked like a room at all.

"Wow!" Abi stood in the doorway, staring at what looked like a forest, right in the middle of Pooch Parlour!

"It's quite something, isn't it?" Aunt Tiffany said, smiling.

"It really is," Abi agreed.

Somehow, Mr Francis's team had turned the room into a fairytale picnic scene. There were trees in pots, with painted screens behind them covered in leaves and vines and a countryside mural. The floor was covered with what looked like real grass. And, in the middle, the doggy-height table Aunt Tiffany used for parties had been covered in a picnic blanket!

"Are those the collars?" Aunt Tiffany asked, and Abi nodded, handing them over. "Great. I'll get these to the Doggy Daycare while you girls help set the table. Mr Francis will be here any minute with the photographer, and the actress playing Sally White."

"Wait!" Polly said, and Aunt Tiffany stopped. "Can I take Pickle's collar, please?"

Aunt Tiffany smiled. "Of course," she said, pulling the smallest collar from the bag.

Polly took it and called, "Pickle!"

Pickle came scampering towards them, the red bow in her topknot bobbing as she ran. She stopped at Polly's feet, and Polly knelt down beside the tiny dog.

"You're a dog star now, Pickle," Polly said, as she fastened the collar around Pickle's neck.

Abi smiled. Even if Pickle didn't get to be in the film itself, at least she would be in the photos. And Abi and Polly had enjoyed training her! Maybe Polly would sign her up to the agency and she could star in Mr Francis's next film.

"Girls? Can you give me a hand here?" Kim asked from the doorway, laden down with a stack of silver bowls. Mel was right behind her with two large bags of the special dog food Mr Francis had selected.

Abi and Polly rushed over to help and between them they laid out seven places at the table. Even the bowls were different sizes, each with a dog's character name engraved on the side.

They had just got everything ready when the door to the party room opened and Aunt Tiffany returned with the seven dogs. A moment later, Mr Francis arrived.

"See, I knew this room would be perfect

for the shoot," Mr Francis said. "What do you think, guys?"

"It looks like it'll work," the photographer agreed. "I'd better get set up."

"Polly? Abi? Come and say hello to our Sally White, the lovely Violet Hayes," Mr Francis said.

Lulu and Pickle, bright red collars shining, followed the girls over to meet the actress.

"You've met my daughter Polly, right? And this is her friend Abi," Mr Francis said. "They've been helping get everything ready for today. Polly will be playing the girl in the park who waves you off on your adventure. And her dog Pickle is even stepping in to save the day for the photo shoot."

The actress smiled at the girls, then bent down to pet the dogs. "They're lovely."

"And Pickle learned a new trick today," Abi said, nudging Polly.

Polly nodded, her head bobbing up and down in excitement. "She did! It's really great, Dad. She's doing so well at her training, just ask the handlers. Can we show you the trick? It won't take long."

"Maybe later," Mr Francis said, glancing over at the photographer, who had already finished setting up his camera and was taking a few test shots. "I think it's time to start."

Polly's shoulders sank and Abi couldn't help but be disappointed too. If only Mr Francis could see how much Pickle had learned in just one day…

"I'll see you later, girls," Violet said.

"Bye," Abi said, a little shyly, and Polly echoed her.

"Wave goodbye, Pickle," Polly said, and Abi held her breath. Would she do it? Could she…

Yes! Abi beamed as the little Yorkie sat down and waved her paw!

Chapter Ten

"She did it!" Abi cried, while Polly fished in her pockets for a treat and made a big fuss of Pickle.

"Of course she did, she's so clever," Polly said.

Violet laughed. "That was the cutest thing I've ever seen! It would be perfect in the film, don't you think, Don?"

Mr Francis shook his head, but he was smiling. "Did you girls teach her to do that this morning?"

"We did," Polly said proudly. "Abi has a book."

Mr Francis turned his attention to Abi and she tried not to fidget under his gaze. "It seems to me that Abi has a knack with dogs too. It wouldn't surprise me if I find her working with the animals on one of my films in a few years' time."

Abi blushed. She hoped so!

"It wouldn't surprise me, either," Aunt Tiffany said, coming over to join them. "It takes a lot of patience and hard work to teach a dog a trick like that in one day."

"We taught Pickle and Lulu to shake hands, first," Abi explained to her aunt. "We were just moving on to waving when the dog stars arrived and we had to stop. That's the first time Pickle managed it perfectly."

"But do you think you could get her to do it again, Polly?" Mr Francis asked. "And to do it every time you asked her to?"

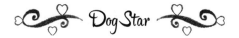

"Definitely," Polly said. "I know just what to do now. All we need is practice."

"Well, in that case..." Mr Francis paused, then grinned. "I think Pickle had better be in the film, waving goodbye to Sally White as she heads off into the woods, don't you!"

"Yes!" Polly shouted, and wrapped her arms around Abi in a huge hug. "We did it!"

The girls bounced up and down, still holding on to each other.

Abi couldn't believe her plan had worked! Now she was more sure than ever about what she wanted to do when she grew up. She would be a world-famous dog trainer, looking after all the dog stars of the future!

But for now, there was still a photo shoot to take care of.

"OK, girls. We'll celebrate afterwards," Mr Francis said. "But first, we need to get this photo shoot on the road!"

Getting all seven dogs to sit down at the table at the same time wasn't easy. The photographer, Quentin, adjusted the lights on tall metal stands that he had placed around the table, while the handlers each led their dog into position.

Abi smiled at Polly as she sat Pickle on a red cushion. Her new friend had a wide, proud smile on her face.

Quentin stepped back and studied the

scene. Then he shook his head. "No. This isn't quite right. Let's move this one" – he pointed to Sam, the Border collie – "over to there..." This time, he pointed to where Charlie had been placed. As their handlers swapped the dogs round, Quentin kept staring intently at the table.

With the dogs in place, everyone looked up at him for approval. But again, he shook his head. "Sorry, guys. Let's try this..."

It took another six moves before Quentin was satisfied. Lulu had grown bored, and wandered off into the corner where Fidget, dressed in a sweater to cover up his bald patches, was playing with a Treat Tumbler – a bobbing, wobbling toy that gave out occasional treats as he played. Before long, both dogs were batting the toy between them, snaffling down the Barker's Bites inside as they tipped out.

Abi smiled. Lulu had got along well with every single dog that had come to Pooch Parlour that day. She might not be a film star, but being able to make friends was equally important.

Meanwhile, Quentin snapped away, catching the dogs in action as they tucked into their picnic. In addition to the silver bowls full of food, Aunt Tiffany had provided specially baked doggy treats shaped like apples and decorated with golden frosting that was safe for dogs to eat. Duke particularly liked those – the Great Dane had wolfed down three while Abi watched!

The food seemed enough to keep the dogs at the table while the photos were taken, but Quentin didn't waste any time. Having got the lights – and dogs – exactly where he wanted them, he darted around the table taking shot after shot from every angle. Abi stood out of the way with Aunt Tiffany as they listened to the camera snapping away.

Then, suddenly, it was over.

"Finished!" Quentin declared, lowering his camera. Everyone seemed to breathe a sigh of relief, and the handlers stopped encouraging the dogs to stay at the table. One by one, the dogs jumped down, wandering off towards their handlers, or finding one of the toys that Aunt Tiffany had in the play area of the room.

Polly and Pickle joined Abi, and Lulu ran over to play with the little Yorkie.

"Do you think you and Pickle will be coming back to Pooch Parlour for grooming when the film starts?" Abi asked.

"Pickle will be, at least once, I suppose. Before we shoot her big scene!"

"And yours," Abi reminded her. Polly seemed more excited about Pickle being in the film than by her own part in it.

Mr Francis, who had been deep in conversation with Quentin, walked over to them. "We're not quite finished yet," he said. "First I want a photo of Polly, Pickle and me with the whole Pooch Parlour team. Everyone here at Pooch Parlour has really saved the day for us, and you're all welcome to visit us on set any time you like."

"Especially Abi and Lulu!" Polly said,

grinning at Abi.

Abi smiled back. Maybe she didn't have to say goodbye to her new friend just yet!

Mr Francis laughed. "Especially Abi and Lulu. And of course we want you *all* to come to the premiere, as our special guests."

Abi thought she might burst with happiness as Quentin took their photo. Working at Pooch Parlour was just getting better and better!

Read an extract from

Passion for Fashion

The Pooch Parlour team is on location at a charity fashion show. When one of the youngest models falls ill, Abi is spotted by the designer and catapulted into the world of catwalks and quick costume changes. But can she handle Boomer, the highly strung pup who will be her modelling partner?

Chapter One

"This," Abi said, pushing open the door with the "Dogs Welcome" sign on it, "is Pooch Parlour!"

"Wow." Emily stared through the open doorway without moving, which made Abi smile. Her best friend had arrived in London last night for a weekend visit. She had already been amazed by Aunt Tiffany's flat, Aunt Tiffany's miniature dachshund, Hugo, and all the different shops near the luxury dog-grooming salon. But it looked like Pooch Parlour itself was the most impressive thing Emily had seen yet!

Abi's bichon frise, Lulu, sneaked through Emily's legs and padded into the parlour, but Emily stayed still.

"You can go in, you know," Abi joked, and

Emily grinned at her before stepping through the doorway.

Emily had picked the best possible weekend to visit, Abi decided. Pooch Parlour was buzzing with activity, as everyone prepared to move off-site to the glamorous – but dog friendly – Pawchester Hotel for the biggest event of the year – the Best Friend for Life Fashion Show. Aunt Tiffany had promised that the girls would be able to watch the fashion show that night, and tomorrow would be doubly busy with appointments, so there'd be lots for them to do.

"Wow! It's incredible," Emily said, as she explored the Pooch Parlour reception area, staring at the photos on the walls of celebrities and their dogs, and the glass cabinets full of sparkly dog accessories.

"It really is," Abi agreed.

"And you get to work here, every day, all

summer." Emily sighed. "You're so lucky."

Abi knew that she was lucky. Not every nine-year-old girl had an aunt who ran a grooming parlour for the pets of the rich and famous, and not every nine-year-old girl got to spend a whole summer helping out there. It was hard work, taking care of the dogs, and doing whatever the Pooch Parlour staff needed her to do – but Abi loved it. And it was good practice for her future dream career, looking after the animals who starred in films and on TV.

"Well, this weekend you get to work here too," Abi said. "Come on, I want to show you around Pooch Parlour."

Read *Passion for Fashion* to find out what happens next!

How to be a Pooch-Pampering Professional!

Dog grooming can be heaps of fun for both you and your pup – but it's important to know the right techniques!

Follow our top tips for the perfect pamper:

Make a Splash!

Some pooches love baths, but for others they can be a bit scary. Try giving your pup treats in the tub, so he or she connects water with having fun.

Brush Up!

A dog's coat needs brushing to keep it glossy. Even if your pup is short-haired like Hugo, regular brushing will help to remove loose dead hairs and keep your pooch's fur slick and clean so they look and feel their best.

Perfect Match!

Find out what kind of brush is right for your breed of dog. A fluff-ball like Jade needs a pin brush, whereas a curved wire brush is best for Lulu's wavy fur. Ask your breeder or local dog-grooming parlour for advice.

Smooth Moves!

Sometimes a dog's fur can get tangled into clumps called "mats", though regular brushing will help prevent this. If your poor pup's coat is matted, ask an adult to help you rub some baby oil into the knots before very gently combing them out with your fingers.

Natural Beauty!

Dogs come in a range of beautiful colours and it's best to keep it that way! Dyeing a dog's fur can cause an allergic reaction, making your pup very uncomfortable. The staff at Pooch Parlour never dye a dog's fur – the pups are gorgeous just as they are!

Did you know...?
Fun facts about Yorkshire Terriers

The smallest dog ever recorded was a Yorkie called Sylvia. She weighed 115g (that's about the same as a small apple!) and measured 9.5cm from the tip of her tail to her nose.

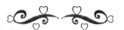

During the first two weeks of their lives, Yorkshire terrier puppies spend 90 per cent of their time sleeping.

A Yorkie called Smoky became a hero during World War II. She was found in the New Guinea jungle and went on many missions. She even jumped from a tower with her very own parachute!

Most modern Yorkies can be traced back to one dog, called Huddersfield Ben. He lived in Yorkshire, England in the nineteenth century and was father to lots of puppies.

If a puppy has a Yorkie as one parent and a Poodle as the other, then they are classified as a Yorkie-Poo!

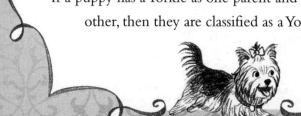

Read them all!

Out in June

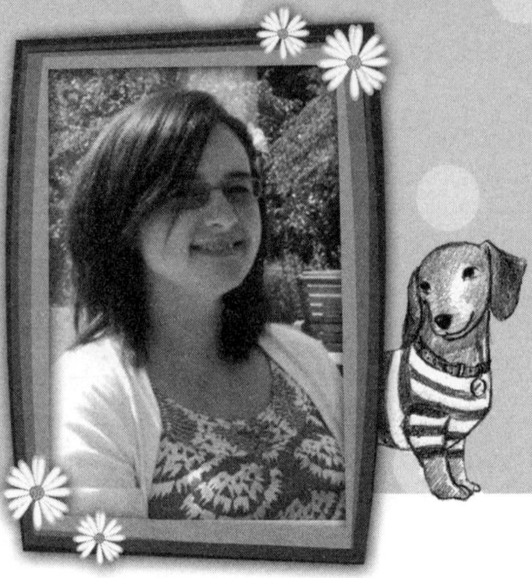

Katy Cannon was born in the United Arab Emirates, grew up in North Wales and now lives in Hertfordshire with her husband and daughter Holly.

Katy loves animals, and grew up with a cat, lots of fish and a variety of gerbils. One of her favourite pastimes is going on holiday to the seaside, where she can paddle in the sea and eat fish and chips!

For more about the author, visit her website:

www.katycannon.com